Hillary Rodham Clinton

Hillary
Rodham
Clinton

By Victoria Sherrow

DILLON PRESS
New York

Maxwell Macmillan Canada
Toronto

Maxwell Macmillan International
New York Oxford Singapore Sydney

Photo Credits

Cover: AP-Wide World Photos
AP-Wide World Photos: 2, 5, 6, 8, 10, 12, 15, 18, 30, 33, 35, 37, 40, 42, 47, 49, 50, 53, 54, 57, 59
Margaret Clapp Library/Wellesley College: 20, 22, 24
Beverly M. Rezneck Photography: 26

Book design by Carol Matsuyama

Library of Congress Cataloging-in-Publication Data

Sherrow, Victoria.
   Hillary Rodham Clinton / by Victoria Sherrow. — 1st ed.
   . p. cm. — (Taking part)
   Summary: A biography of the lawyer, activist, and First Lady of the United States.
   ISBN 0-87518-621-1
   1. Clinton, Hillary Rodham—Juvenile literature. 2. Clinton, Bill, 1946- —Juvenile literature. 3. Presidents—United States—Wives—Biography—Juvenile literature. [1. Clinton, Hillary Rodham. 2. First ladies.] I. Title. II. Series.
   E887.C55S48   1993
   973.929'092—dc20
   [B]   93-7806

Dillon Press   Maxwell Macmillan Canada, Inc.
Macmillan Publishing Company   1200 Eglinton Avenue East
866 Third Avenue   Suite 200
New York, NY 10022   Don Mills, Ontario M3C 3N1

Macmillan Publishing Company is part of the Maxwell Communication Group of Companies.

First edition

Printed in the United States of America

10   9   8   7   6   5   4   3   2   1

SCOTT

Contents

Introduction

When Arkansas governor Bill Clinton was campaigning for president in 1992, his wife, Hillary, got a lot of attention, too. Besides being a wife and mother, Hillary Rodham Clinton was a successful lawyer. She had been named one of the 100 most influential attorneys in the country. For more than 20 years, Hillary had worked hard to improve conditions for children and families in Arkansas and all over America.

People said that Governor Bill Clinton valued his wife's opinion on major issues. At his request, Hillary had headed a large committee to help improve Arkansas's public schools. The press also reported that Hillary earned more money as a lawyer than her husband earned as governor. Bill Clinton did not seem to mind. He spoke often, and with pride, about his wife's talents and achievements. During the campaign, Governor Clinton said that if he were elected, Americans would get "two for the price of one."

Hillary waves to the crowd during a campaign stop in Cleveland, Ohio.

An active member of Bill Clinton's team, Hillary speaks with senators George Mitchell (left) *and Edward Kennedy* (right) *about policy issues.*

On January 20, 1993, Bill Clinton became the nation's 42nd president. Again people wondered about Hillary: What kind of first lady would she be? She was the first "working mother" ever to live in the White House and was a public figure in her own right. Would she play a larger role in government than former presidents' wives? One journalist asked, "Can she bring home the bacon and still serve tea and cookies?"

That is just what Hillary had been doing for years. Her husband and friends praise the way she has fulfilled the many roles in her life—as wife, mother, lawyer, first lady of Arkansas, and public servant. Hillary has said that she sees life as "a balance of family, work, and service." She claims that like other women today, she faces big challenges and has to juggle many roles.

From the start, Hillary Clinton said she wanted to

keep helping children, whom she calls "America's most unprotected citizens." She said that her main goal in the White House was "to implement my husband's agenda for families and children, which would be a real opportunity to zero in on issues I have worked on for twenty years."

But Hillary's concern for others had started years earlier, long before she became a lawyer. As she grew up in Illinois, her religion and family influenced her to care about other people. When she was a teenager, Hillary raised money and organized baby-sitting services for families of migrant workers who labored on nearby farms. She believed that with so many blessings in her own life, she should contribute something to the community.

It seemed clear that Hillary would bring the same energy and commitment to the White House that she had shown throughout her life. Shortly before moving to Washington, she said, "It is very important that I try to do the very best job that I can do. It is something that I've thought a lot about. . . . I want to make a difference."

CHAPTER 1 Growing Up in the Midwest

After the 1992 presidential election, Hillary Clinton's two younger brothers talked about growing up in the Rodham household. Hugh said that the family values were clear: public service and compassion. "I think that shows in all our work now. Hillary with her Children's Defense Fund, me with my public defender stuff, and Tony with what he's done for poor people in this county [Dade County, Florida]."

Asked what big sister Hillary was like as a child, both brothers agreed she had been a tough act to follow in school. Tony added, "When she wasn't studying, she was a lot of fun."

Hillary Rodham was born on October 26, 1947. She and brothers Hugh (born in 1950) and Tony (born in 1954) grew up in Park Ridge, a suburb of Chicago, Illinois. The family lived in a comfortable two-story brick home. Hillary's father, Hugh, Sr., owned a drapery fabric business. Her mother, Dorothy, worked as a

Hillary takes a break from the fast pace of life in Washington to walk along the beach.

An avid reader ever since she was young, Hillary shares a story with a kindergarten class.

full-time homemaker and mother.

Dorothy Rodham called her daughter a bright, responsible child. "I never had to worry about Hillary putting her finger in a light socket or anything. I had great confidence in that child," she said.

As a child, Hillary enjoyed playing with her brothers and other friends. The Rodhams and many families of that time did not own a television set until the mid- to late 1950s. So there was plenty of time for creativity and make-believe activities. With other children, Hillary played ball, rode her bicycle, and went to local parks. Often she was in charge of watching Hugh and Tony.

Hillary was athletic. She liked softball and volleyball and played on organized teams when she was a teenager. Baseball, tennis, and swimming were favorite summer pastimes. In the winter, ice-skating on local ponds was followed by steamy cups of hot chocolate. Hillary also took ballet and piano lessons. In elementary school, she joined a Brownie Scout troop. Later she became a Girl Scout and worked to earn all the merit badges that were available.

Growing up, Hillary considered several future careers. At one time, she thought about becoming an astronaut. She wrote a letter to the National Aeronautics and Space Administration (NASA) asking them how she might go about it. Their reply stated they were "not taking any girls." Hillary remembers being annoyed. She later said, "I couldn't believe it." She was pleased when NASA changed its policy and Sally Ride and other women became successful astronauts.

It was a wonderful home life, according to Hillary and her brothers. Her parents kissed each other good-bye every morning before Hugh, Sr., left for work. There was plenty of food, and there were nice clothes and some luxuries, like music lessons and summer vacations. The children felt loved and secure. Hillary's brother Hugh said they had "typical Midwestern values . . . church on Sunday, respect your elders, do well in school, participate in sports."

Hugh, Sr., and Dorothy Rodham made a special effort to help their children appreciate their advantages. Both of Hillary's parents had lived through hard economic times during the Great Depression of the 1930s. Hugh, Sr., had grown up in Scranton, Pennsylvania, where his father worked in a lace factory. As a young man, he had spent time digging coal in the dank mines.

When visiting her father's hometown, Hillary and her brothers saw the mines. Their parents also showed them the slum areas around Chicago where many people experienced poverty and hardships. Hillary's brother

Hillary and Tipper Gore, wife of Vice President Al Gore, visit a working-class steel town.

Hugh later said, "They wanted us to find out the plight of other people."

Hillary and her brothers worked for their pocket money. "We were probably the only kids in the whole suburb who didn't get an allowance. We'd rake the leaves, cut the grass, pull weeds, shovel snow," Tony Rodham said of those days. They held dandelion-pulling contests in the yard, earning a penny for each dandelion.

Hillary said that her parents gave her encouragement and support with school and other activities. Her father also prodded her toward excellence. He would read her report cards and ask her if she was sure she had done her very best. His attitude, says Hillary, was, "You did well, but could you do better? It's hard out there."

Besides her family, Hillary was strongly influenced by religion. She took part in church activities and read books by religious thinkers, including Dietrich Bonhoeffer and Søren Kierkegaard. The Reverend Don Jones led Hillary's youth group at the First Methodist Church. He recalled that she was "fun-loving and very gregarious." The group often discussed social problems and values people should strive to live by. "What my church taught me is, because I had those blessings from my family, I owed something back," Hillary later said.

During her teens, she tried to help less fortunate people. She started a baby-sitting service for the children of Mexican migrant workers. These people spent long hours picking crops at farms about three blocks from Hillary's neighborhood. With very low wages, they lived in poverty and suffered from poor housing and little, if any, health care. Hillary and some of her friends took part in church fund-raising efforts on their behalf.

Hillary Rodham was aware of racial injustice as well as poverty. The black civil rights movement was expanding during the 1950s and 1960s when she was a teenager. Newspapers and television reported the struggle of black Americans to get rid of racism and discrimination in jobs, voting, housing, education, and public accommodations. Hillary heard a speech by civil rights leader Dr. Martin Luther King, Jr., in 1962 when she was 15 years old.

At Maine South High School, Hillary was active in many activities. She dressed like other teenage girls of her day in pleated or A-line skirts, neat blouses with bows or rounded collars, vests, sweaters, knee socks, and loafers. Her dark blond hair was sometimes pulled up into a ponytail. As a junior, she sang in a variety show and was vice president of her class. Her summer job was as a lifeguard at the town's municipal pool.

Hillary also showed her interest in politics and social

Hillary and Bill Clinton visit Hillary's high school in Illinois during the presidential campaign.

issues at school. She was on the student council and was often a class officer, although she lost a bid for senior class president. She was a member of the National Honor Society, a group that included top students, and shone on the debating team. When she graduated, she won many honors, including the first social science prize ever given by Maine South High School.

At that time, and even today, some girls worried that boys might not like them if they seemed too smart. Hillary was more straightforward. She chose not to hide her intelligence. When she had an opinion or idea, she wanted to express herself. She once said that her parents, teachers, and preachers had made her feel that "I could do what I set my mind to do and they would be there for me." Her mother told Hillary not to base her future plans on other people's ideas about which roles were right for girls and which for boys.

Bright and accomplished, Hillary Rodham had her choice of colleges. She picked the renowned Wellesley College and set off in the fall of 1965. At 17 she was ready for new challenges in a different region of the country: New England.

CHAPTER 2 # College Days

In the fall of 1965, Hillary Rodham became a freshman at Wellesley College near Boston, Massachusetts. Wellesley belonged to a prestigious group of all-women's schools often called the "Seven Sisters." The students were expected to behave properly and to join the faculty on Thursday afternoons for dressy teas.

Because Hillary was preparing for a career in law, she took many courses in political science, the study of political institutions, laws, and government. She also focused on psychology, the study of human personality and development.

The civil rights movement that had interested Hillary during her teens continued to expand in the mid-1960s. President Lyndon Johnson had signed into law the 1964 Civil Rights Act that protected voting rights and said that all Americans should have "full and equal enjoyment of the goods, services, facilities, privileges, advantages, and accommodations of any place of public

First lady-to-be Hillary Rodham splashes in a lake near Wellesley.

accommodation." It forbade school segregation and discrimination against people in any federal job or program.

When Hillary was in college, Dr. Martin Luther King, Jr., and other civil rights leaders continued to draw attention to the problems that faced black Americans. Many people worked to make sure that black citizens were not prevented by force or harassment from voting.

As a sophomore, Hillary joined some other students in asking school officials to bring more black students to Wellesley.

Hillary was horrified when Martin Luther King, Jr., was assassinated in April 1968, as she was finishing her junior year of college. Her roommate later said that she was "completely distraught about the horror of it." Hillary was usually calm and private with her feelings. People had seldom seen her so upset.

But life wasn't always serious for Hillary Rodham. Her classmates recalled how she showed her sense of individuality for a school dance during her third year. She wore bright orange culottes (a divided skirt) with feathers and lots of bracelets. It was a daring outfit compared to the neat, traditional clothing usually worn at Wellesley.

For her senior thesis, Hillary chose to write about poverty and community development. A major part of her paper was devoted to the ways in which people take responsibility for their lives. Communities could organize themselves and work together to resolve problems.

John R. Quarles, Chairman of the Board of Trustees; Hillary Rodham; Ruth M. Adams, President of Wellesley; and Senator Edward Brook, commencement speaker, at Hillary's graduation from Wellesley.

As a senior, Hillary Rodham was chosen by her classmates to read a speech at their graduation exercises. It was the first time a student had ever had the chance to speak in this way. Hillary talked about idealism and how it had affected her generation. The graduating seniors gave her a standing ovation. Parts of her speech were later quoted in *Life* magazine. She graduated in 1969 with high academic honors.

Hillary was accepted at several law schools and chose

to attend Yale Law School in New Haven, Connecticut. One of her Wellesley professors wrote a letter of recommendation, calling her "the most able student" he'd encountered in his years of teaching. He said that he believed Hillary Rodham was going to "make a strong contribution to American society."

Her goal in gaining a law degree was to use her career to serve people who needed help. Just one month after Hillary entered Yale Law School, she met someone who would influence her role as a children's advocate for years to come. She was Marian Wright Edelman, who had graduated from Yale Law School six years earlier. Edelman had married, become a mother, and started the Washington Research Project (which later became the Children's Defense Fund). The project worked hard to expand Head Start programs.

Head Start had begun as part of President Johnson's war on poverty during the mid-1960s. It offered free preschool to four-year-old children whose families could not afford private preschools. Head Start worked with the children and their families to help get them ready for school. It also tried to meet their other needs, including health, nutrition, and social services.

Hillary heard Marian Wright Edelman speak about how terribly neglected many American children were. Afterward, Hillary met Mrs. Edelman and asked her if she could work for the Washington Research Project during the summer. Hillary seemed well qualified and sincere. But Mrs. Edelman told her, regretfully, that the project could not afford to pay summer law interns. Hillary said she would work there free, which she did the next summer.

In 1971 another big event happened in Hillary's life: She met her future husband. Bill Clinton was also a law student at Yale. The Clintons have said that they met in the law library. Bill Clinton said he was talking to another law student about the *Yale Law Review*. "And all this time I was talking to this guy about the *Law Review*, I was looking at Hillary at the other end of the library. And the Yale Law School Library is a real long, narrow [room]. She was down at the other end. . . . I was just staring at her while this guy was looking at a book, and

Hillary and Bill Clinton with Marian Wright Edelman, Hillary's longtime hero.

she closed this book, and she walked all the way down the library . . . and she came up to me and she said, 'Look, if you're going to keep staring at me, and I'm going to keep staring back, I think we should at least know each other. I'm Hillary Rodham. What's your name?'"

As they got acquainted, they found they shared many interests and goals. Bill Clinton later said, "I remember being genuinely afraid of falling in love with Hillary, because she was so gifted and so special. I was a serious student, but she was a brain, a presence."

They also had something else in common. Although

Hillary Rodham Clinton

Hillary had grown up as a Republican and had supported the party when she entered college, she was now a Democrat. Bill had been a Democrat his entire life. In 1972 she and Bill went to work for the presidential campaign of George McGovern. McGovern was the Democratic candidate running against the Republican, President Richard Nixon. Bill Clinton was in charge of the campaign in Texas. Hillary worked there with him during the fall. Although they were away from their classes during that time, they kept up with their coursework and got good grades on their exams.

For her law thesis, a major paper students have to write before graduating, Hillary wrote about the rights of children. She had been working with disadvantaged children at Yale–New Haven Hospital, as well as continuing her work with Marian Wright Edelman's group. She graduated from Yale Law School with honors.

After her 1973 graduation, Hillary went to Washington, D.C., to work as a staff attorney for Edelman's organization. In 1974 she worked for the House Judiciary Committee impeachment staff during the Watergate hearings. One of her professors at Yale had recommended her for this job.

The hearings took place after it was learned that high-ranking members of President Nixon's staff had arranged a burglary at Democratic headquarters in the Watergate Hotel in Washington. A congressional committee was set up to investigate any misconduct by the president. Nixon might have been impeached—charged with wrongdoing and forced out of office—if that were the case. But in August 1974 he resigned from office. Vice President Gerald Ford became president.

Bill Clinton was in Hillary's thoughts during this time. When she finished her work with the Judiciary Committee, she received several attractive offers to work for law firms in Washington, D.C., and New York City. But Bill's roots were in Arkansas, and he had returned there to teach law. He had hoped Hillary would join him. Hillary later recalled that she kept thinking, as she tried to decide what job she would take next, that there was something special about Bill Clinton.

CHAPTER 3 A New Life in Arkansas

In the end, Hillary decided to "follow my heart to Arkansas," as she later put it. Some friends and family members were surprised that she had turned down the other high-paying jobs that she could have taken. But Hillary said it was "something I had to do." She packed her 10-speed bike, 20 boxes of books, and other belongings into a friend's 1968 Buick and moved across the country. Hillary began teaching in Fayetteville, at the University of Arkansas Law School, as Bill Clinton was doing. He had also run for the state congress in 1974 and had nearly won.

Bill was delighted when Hillary joined him at the law school. Hillary enjoyed living in the small Arkansas town. She later said she had quickly felt at home and liked both the school and the other teachers. During her first year of teaching, she and Bill talked about getting married.

During August 1975, Hillary left Fayetteville to visit

Hillary and Bill Clinton in the early days of their marriage some friends. When she got back, Bill took her for a ride and pointed to a small house with a bay window next to a lake. The couple had once driven by the house and Hillary had admired it. Now Bill said, "Well, I thought you liked it, so I bought it. So I guess we'll have to get married now."

The marriage ceremony was held on October 11, 1975. Hillary wore a high-waisted, Victorian-style linen dress with a tiered skirt that she had found in a local department store. It was a quiet wedding attended by 20 people, mostly their families. Bill's half-brother, Roger, was his best man. The rings the couple gave each other were treasured family heirlooms. More than 100 people joined them for a backyard reception. Then the couple enjoyed a honeymoon in sunny Acapulco, Mexico.

Hillary decided to keep using Hillary Rodham as her professional name. Many women made that choice during the 1970s and in the years thereafter. The 1970s marked a growth in the women's rights movement that stressed more choices for women and equality in the workplace.

Married since 1975, Hillary and Bill have supported each other's careers while still keeping the focus on their relationship.

The newlyweds had happy times in their first house. They enjoyed entertaining friends. Hillary remembered evenings of "long conversations with friends and dinners that went on for hours where you talked about everything in your life and in the world."

Then Bill's political career took the Clintons to Little Rock, the capital of Arkansas. Hillary taught at the law school there. She directed the school's legal aid clinic, where low-income people got free or inexpensive legal help. Bill ran for attorney general in 1976 and won. Besides teaching, Hillary represented children as a courtroom lawyer. She was not paid for much of her public work.

In 1977 Hillary Rodham accepted a position as an associate at the Rose Law Firm, Little Rock's most prestigious group of attorneys.

Now she had her work at the firm in addition to her advocacy work. She was also helping Bill in his new campaign. He had gained a good reputation as a hard-working attorney general. Now he wanted to become governor of Arkansas. In 1978 Hillary was named to the board of directors of the Children's Defense Fund, headed by Marian Wright Edelman. The Children's Defense Fund had grown out of the Washington Research Project and aimed to address the many needs of America's children.

Bill defeated four rivals to become the youngest governor in Arkansas history. On January 10, 1979, Hillary stood next to her husband as he was sworn in to

Bill and Hillary attend a dinner at the White House during Bill's first term as Governor of Arkansas.

office. She was now first lady of Arkansas at age 31. For the inaugural ball, Hillary wore a long, deep-red velvet dress made by a local designer. It was a copy of her old-fashioned wedding gown. The couple moved into the spacious red-brick governor's mansion.

Bill Clinton's inaugural address had stressed his desire to improve public education and health care in Arkansas. These issues concerned Hillary, too. Her career as an attorney was progressing. She was promoted to a partnership in the Rose Law Firm during Bill's first year as governor.

In 1979 the Clintons were delighted to find out that Hillary was expecting a baby. She was careful to eat well and do everything she could to have a healthy child. Hillary did not stop working while she was pregnant but did cut back on her hours. She took some time off around the time the baby was born. The men at her firm were not used to seeing a pregnant lawyer, so Hillary tried to put them at ease.

On February 27, 1980, Chelsea Victoria Clinton was born. Hillary and Bill chose her name from a song they

Hillary attends the MTV Ball with Chelsea. Hillary has always tried to keep Chelsea's best interests in mind when making decisions about the family.

both loved, "Chelsea Morning." The song was written by Canadian-born folksinger Joni Mitchell. Judy Collins, one of the Clintons' favorite singers, had recorded it. Baby Chelsea brought her parents great joy. They liked caring for her and watching her grow and develop.

While Bill faced the many challenges of his job, Hillary was busy as an attorney, children's advocate, wife, and mother. Keeping up with so many activities took careful organization. Hillary also made time to stay in touch with close friends. She was known as a friendly first lady. Sometimes she greeted guests at the governor's mansion herself. She could be seen wearing casual clothes like blue jeans.

Life in the governor's mansion had certain comforts and conveniences for the Clintons. They had a staff of people to keep things clean and in order. There was a place for a live-in baby-sitter to help care for Chelsea.

But Bill's term as governor was not going as well as he had hoped. Some people in Arkansas were upset when he increased the fees for auto and truck licenses to pay for highway improvements. Some of the state's physicians did not like the health clinics he set up in rural areas. Higher taxes on corporations upset many businessmen. Bill's proposals for changing the schools were popular with some people but opposed by others.

The Republicans campaigned hard against Bill Clinton in the 1980 campaign. They talked about Hillary, too, saying that it was odd that she did not use her husband's last name. More traditional voters thought married women should not keep their maiden names.

Bill was narrowly defeated in the November 1980 election. With Hillary beside him holding nine-month-old Chelsea, he said good-bye to the Arkansas congress and prepared to leave office. The Clintons were sad to leave without having finished work that was important to them. They moved into another new house and built their lives away from state government. But Bill was determined to serve again as governor. He and Hillary decided he would run in the next election.

About a year after that, Bill began speaking to the voters in televised ads. He apologized for any mistakes and told people he had learned a great deal. Bill's

Hillary and Bill celebrating Bill's 1982 victory in the race for Governor of Arkansas

political advisers told Hillary she should use her husband's last name. Hillary did not mind doing so. In her private life, she had been viewed as "Mrs. Bill Clinton" or "Hillary Clinton" anyway. She later explained, "It meant more to them [the voters] than it did to me."

Bill was elected governor again in 1982. (He would be reelected five times, serving until he became president in 1992.) The family returned to the red-brick mansion with Chelsea, now a lively, blue-eyed two-year-old. This time, Bill Clinton planned to go more slowly in making changes he thought were needed. Hillary would have important new roles improving education and health care in Arkansas.

CHAPTER 4 # Rewarding Years

Governor Bill Clinton knew that Hillary could handle important tasks. He asked her to head the Arkansas Education Standards Committee, an unpaid job leading the group that would set standards for the public schools. Hillary visited schools and held meetings to hear people's ideas about education. She spoke with teachers, principals, and parents all over Arkansas.

Then her committee made recommendations. It suggested smaller numbers of students per teacher and said teachers should take competency tests. Some teachers protested and said they would not take the tests. After a heated debate, the state congress passed this law. Other states have adopted a similar policy.

Hillary had long thought that children must be *ready* for school when they start. She found a program that had been used to help parents teach their preschool children skills that lead to success: HIPPY (Home Instruction Program for Preschool Youth) International. Hillary

As the wife of the governor, Hillary Clinton was very active in the political life of Arkansas.

brought the program to disadvantaged families in Arkansas. Volunteers taught parents how to obtain free books and other materials. An extra benefit of the program was that parents grew more self-confident. They felt good about helping their children. Some parents decided to get more education themselves.

Besides that, Hillary served on the board of directors for the Arkansas Children's Hospital. She promoted child health care and worked for the Southern Governors' Association Task Force on Infant Mortality. Arkansas did not have a neonatal care unit, a hospital unit for newborns who needed special care because they were sick or very premature. Hillary organized the first one in the state. She helped to start a helicopter service called Angel One. It flew around Arkansas taking health care to patients who needed emergency help.

While doing these important public jobs, Hillary was still working at the Rose Law Firm. She continued to serve on the board of the Children's Defense Fund and always attended its meetings. Besides, she served as a member of other boards, including those of Wal-Mart and the Children's Television Network.

Daughter Chelsea was growing up during those years in the governor's mansion. Bill took her to school each day, and Hillary was with her for many activities. Hillary once said, "There's nothing more important to me than my daughter." In her blue Oldsmobile, Hillary drove Chelsea to dance lessons and ball games. Like other parents, she went to school plays and dance recitals. Together she and Chelsea shopped at the grocery store on Saturdays. When Chelsea got older, she attended the Methodist church with Hillary. Bill worshiped at a Baptist church, keeping his own religious heritage.

The family enjoyed evenings of playing card games, like hearts and gin rummy. They played a game called Pictionary together and ate take-out pizza, a family favorite. Some nights were spent at the movies. When Hillary had to travel away from home, she made Chelsea videotapes of herself and left her notes and surprises.

By the late 1980s, Bill Clinton had gained a reputation as a governor who had worked hard for education. He headed a national governor's task force on education. In 1987 the American Bar Association, a national lawyer's group, asked Hillary to serve on its Commission on Women in the Profession. She studied special problems faced by women lawyers.

For years Bill had thought about running for president. He and Hillary discussed whether he should try to become the Democratic nominee in 1992. It would demand a great deal of time and effort from them both. Bill would be challenging President George Bush, who was very popular in 1990 when Bill and others began to think about running.

Even so, Bill and Hillary decided to try. The presidency offered unique chances to do things for America that they both felt were important.

It was a strenuous campaign. Several Democratic candidates besides Bill hoped to win the party's nomination. He worked hard to get enough votes in the state primary elections. As the primaries went on in 1992, Bill became the leader. By the end, he had won enough primaries to be nominated by the Democratic convention held in June.

Hillary greets an enthusiastic supporter after finishing a speech.

Before the presidential election, Bill traveled all over America for debates, speeches, and other appearances. Hillary did lots of campaigning, too. During that time, she was concerned about meeting Chelsea's needs. The Clintons thought she should lead as normal a life as possible, without publicity. Hillary went back to Arkansas every three or four days. She was glad her parents had moved to Little Rock and were caring for Chelsea. While traveling, Hillary could still check Chelsea's schoolwork—by fax machine! Friends said that despite her hectic schedule, Hillary was generous with her time.

As the election grew near, Hillary was criticized by people who did not want Bill Clinton to be elected. Friends said she was sad and hurt about the untrue or misleading things people said about her. Sometimes they took a few sentences out of papers she had written and quoted those pieces alone. This gave a false picture of her ideas. Hillary thought some people stressed her career as a lawyer with strong political opinions but did not also show her as wife, mother, or first lady of Arkansas.

At times, Hillary said things during the campaign that were misunderstood. Once someone asked her why she had pursued her career. Hillary said, "I suppose I could have stayed home and baked cookies and had teas, but what I decided to do is fulfill my profession. The work that I have done as a professional, a public advocate, has been aimed . . . to assure that women can make the choices . . . whether it's a full-time career, full-time motherhood, or some combination."

Tipper Gore, Chelsea Clinton, and Hillary Clinton—three women very central to the presidential campaign.

When the press reported her comment about "baking cookies," some people thought Hillary was criticizing homemakers or even baking itself. Hillary tried to explain what she meant. And she assured people that she had baked plenty of cookies in her life. She shared some recipes, too. One of her favorites was chocolate-chip oatmeal cookies that were a Rodham Christmas tradition. After these experiences, Hillary was careful not to say things that could be cut into small pieces called

Hillary helps out at a New York bakery.

"sound bites" for TV or news shows.

Hillary thought that some of the criticism of her occurred because Americans were still trying to adjust to the changing roles of men and women. She was the first candidate's wife to have had a career as significant as her husband's. The public talked about this and about how women's roles had changed since the 1950s.

Still, it was frustrating. She said, "The rules that prevail all too often in our society go something like this:

If you grow up and you don't get married and you don't have children, you're an oddball. If you get married and don't have children, you're a selfish yuppie. If you get married, have children, and go out into the work world as well, you're a bad mother. And if you get married, have children, and stay at home, you've wasted your education."

People also commented on Hillary's hairdo, clothing, and appearance. They noticed when her hair seemed a lighter shade of blond and when she went from wearing headbands to a shorter style of hair. In past elections, candidates' wives had gone through the same kind of scrutiny. Hillary said she did not understand why people wasted time discussing her hair and clothes when vital issues were at stake. She said people should focus on "what will matter in their own lives."

Hillary kept her positive attitude and continued to talk about issues like education and health care. She later said, "You have to learn to take political attacks seriously but not personally, so that you don't let them interfere with what you are."

During a fun moment in the campaign, Hillary appeared at Penn State University, where her father and brother Hugh had graduated. Members of their fraternity gave Hillary a bouquet of roses and a sweatshirt. It read: "For the first woman president—Chelsea."

During the fall, polls of American voters showed that Bill Clinton was leading. The Clintons and vice presidential candidate, Tennessee Senator Al Gore, and his wife, Tipper, continued to campaign hard. They traveled by bus together to speak in different towns. Hillary and Tipper became friends and enjoyed talking and joking together. From time to time, Hillary and Bill had a few moments alone, sneaking out to a movie or enjoying Chinese food.

On November 3, the exhausting campaign ended. Bill Clinton was elected president. Hillary looked radiant as she stood beside him and the Gores on Election Night at a rally in Little Rock. She and Bill danced as "Don't Stop," a song by the rock group Fleetwood Mac, played. The song and its lyrics had become a symbol of the Clinton campaign. "Don't stop thinking about

Hillary and Bill Clinton and Al and Tipper Gore hold hands in celebration on Election Night.

tomorrow," it said. Bill spoke to the triumphant crowd about the "high hopes and brave hearts" of the American people. Hillary also spoke, thanking voters and supporters. After months of hard work, sacrifices, and countless public appearances, she and Bill had achieved a hard-won victory. Now they faced enormous challenges and opportunities.

CHAPTER 5 # First Partners

The months after the election were hectic. Hillary had a great deal of work to do and she wanted the family to have a wonderful last Christmas in the governor's mansion. She watched Chelsea dance in a performance of *The Nutcracker* ballet and act in a school play, Charles Dickens's *A Christmas Carol.* As usual, the Clintons "adopted" another family that needed help at Christmastime. Hillary said, "We get things they need and deliver them, usually on Christmas Eve. We started doing that with Chelsea a long time ago. And we also try to go by some of the shelters in town and visit with the people there and try to give them some things that are real Christmassy—especially the children, but the adults as well. And we go to church on Christmas Eve as well as Christmas Day. Christmas is really important to us."

There was also much work to do before the move to the White House in January. Many decisions had to be made, including how to transport Socks, the family's

Hillary and Bill share a special moment after learning that Bill captured the Democratic nomination for President.

black and white cat that Chelsea had adopted two years earlier. Hillary had to choose the clothes she would wear during the inauguration and the various parties. She had to conclude work at her law firm before leaving Little Rock.

As Bill Clinton began choosing his staff members, journalists asked Hillary if he had asked for her advice. She said, "I have been consulted and been answering his requests for advice on all of the Cabinet positions." What kind of first lady would Hillary be? Some people, including her mother, Dorothy, compared her to Eleanor Roosevelt. Hillary saw that as a compliment. She said, "Her strength of character and persistence and intelligence and compassion were just remarkable. She was just outstanding in her willingness to look issues squarely in the face and take them on, and she withstood withering criticism from all kinds of people."

Inauguration Day was January 20, 1993. Hillary looked proud and happy as she held a family Bible on which Bill would recite his oath of office. They walked down Pennsylvania Avenue for the traditional parade.

Bill and Hillary toast their success.

That night, there was a series of balls honoring the new president and his wife. The next day, the Clintons awoke in the White House. They had decided to hold an open house and greet visitors from around the nation. When the celebrating was over, Hillary and Bill got right to work.

On January 25, President Clinton announced he had appointed Hillary to head the President's Task Force on Health Care. The task force's job was to design legislation that would make health care available to all Americans and reduce costs. The *New York Times* called it "the most powerful official post ever assigned to a First Lady." President Clinton said he wanted Hillary to do this job because she knew how to organize and lead people to examine complex problems.

Health care had been a top issue during the election. In February 1992 Hillary began visiting hospitals and holding meetings in different cities to discuss health care problems and solutions. She said her committee would look at ways to reduce the high costs of care, including ways to prevent illness. Prevention, such as making sure children got their immunizations, is cheaper in the long run.

Hillary said changing the many different parts of the health care system would be difficult. There were a number of people and organizations involved in delivering health care. Some groups in the system would probably resist changes that reduced their profits or choices. But it was a job that needed to be done, and Hillary was ready to tackle it.

"Woman of the Year."

Early in February, Hillary planned her first official White House dinner. She said the Clintons would use American rather than foreign recipes: "We are trying to move toward healthy, fresh American food." Guests at that dinner ate shrimp, roast tenderloin of beef, baby vegetables in baskets made of zucchini squash, a salad with cheese from Massachusetts, and apple sherbet with a sauce. American wines from three states were served.

A big family event took place that same month. On February 27, Chelsea celebrated her 13th birthday. Chelsea was now an eighth-grader at a private school in Washington. The press reported that she was playing on the soccer team and had invited some girls to a sleepover at the White House. She had also had a scavenger hunt for about 30 friends.

Ever since Hillary herself was 13, people have told her she should run for public office. But she says, "What I see for myself is a role as an advocate." She said that government jobs are best done by people like her husband.

In April, Hillary was saddened by the death of her father. For several weeks, she did not make many public appearances. But she quickly returned to her activities, and seemed more determined than ever to fight for all the causes her father had taught her to believe in.

About her future, Hillary has said, "Depending on how my life unfolds, I would like to go back to teaching, but on a high-school or college level. I like going into high schools. I'm interested in children that age." After the years in Washington, she hopes "to be able to point to *real* progress. I'd like to be able to say there are fewer children in poverty, fewer children going without health care and missing immunizations."

Before moving to the White House, Hillary read about past first ladies. "I've learned that each one has tried to do what she thought was best for her husband and her family and the country as she saw her obligations. And that almost without exception, every one was criticized for something by somebody. If you lived your life trying to make sure that nobody ever criticized you, you would probably never get out of bed—and then you would be criticized for that," she says with dry humor.

President Bill Clinton said that America would soon see that Hillary was "a first lady of many talents." Hillary Rodham Clinton can point with pride to years of service and contributions to society, especially for children. As first lady, she works hard to blend traditional roles as wife, mother, and hostess with her work on important national issues. It is a richly satisfying life that embodies her cherished ideals—"family, work, and service."

Index

About the Author

Before becoming a full-time writer, Victoria Sherrow worked in the field of community mental health. She is the author of more than 30 books for young people, including *Cities at War: Amsterdam*, *Challenges in Education*, *Separation of Church and State*, and *Image and Substance: The Media in U.S. Elections*. Her other biographies include books about Phillis Wheatley, Jonas Salk, Mahatma Gandhi, and Bill Clinton.

The author lives in Connecticut with her husband, Peter Karoczkai, and their three children.